© 1992 The Walt Disney Company

No portion of this book may be reproduced
without the written consent of The Walt Disney Company.

Produced by Kroha Associates, Inc.
Middletown, Connecticut

Illustrated by Yakovetic Productions

Written by M.C. Varley

Printed in the United States of America.

ISBN 1-56326-166-9

A Dragon's Tail

One day, while Sebastian the crab was weeding his garden, Scales stopped by for a visit. "That looks like fun," the dragon said. "Can I try?"

"I'd be happy to have you help me," replied Sebastian. "You can use that hoe over there."

The tiny crab was very grateful to Scales for offering to help. Sebastian had been working hard all morning, and he was getting tired. But as Scales turned to pick up the hoe, his huge tail whipped around behind him and smashed into all of the vegetables in Sebastian's garden!

Carrots and radishes and tomatoes went flying everywhere. "Stop!" cried Sebastian. "You're ruining my garden!" Scales quickly lifted his tail out of the way — and knocked Sebastian right into the lagoon!

"I'm sorry," Scales said as he pulled Sebastian out of the water. "It was an accident. I'll help you clean everything up."

"I think you've 'helped' enough for one day," the crab replied gruffly. But when he saw the sad look on his friend's face, he felt sorry for him. "I know you didn't do it on purpose," Sebastian told him, "but maybe it would be better if *I* did the gardening by *myself*."

As Sebastian went back to work in his garden, Scales slowly walked off toward the Little Mermaid's cove. When he got there he found Ariel and Scuttle preparing a picnic. "Would you like to join us?" the Little Mermaid asked. "We have grapes, oranges and coconuts, and some seaweed sandwiches, too!"

"I'd love to!" Scales said excitedly. But as he sat down his tail bumped into Ariel's picnic basket and sent it sailing out into the water.

"There's nothing I hate more than a soggy seaweed sandwich," squawked Scuttle. "You ought to be more careful with that tail. It's always getting in the way."

"Scuttle! That's not nice!" scolded Ariel. "Scales didn't mean to ruin our picnic."

"Scuttle's right," Scales cried. "My tail *is* always getting in the way! I can't do *anything* right!"

"That's not true," replied Ariel. "There are lots of things you do very well."

"Name one," Scales pouted, feeling very sorry for himself.

"Well, there are so many things, I don't know where to begin," stammered Ariel. "What I mean is —"

"See?" Scales said. "You can't think of anything either!" With that he turned and walked away, dragging his huge tail behind him.

"Scuttle!" whispered Ariel. "Think of something, quick!"
Scuttle thought and thought. "You're very good at being green!"
he called out at last.
"I may be green," the dragon replied, "but I sure feel blue."

"We have to think of a way to help Scales feel better about himself," Ariel told everyone later that afternoon. "He thinks he can't do anything right because his tail always gets in the way."

"Well, it does cause problems," replied Sebastian. "This morning he nearly ruined my garden."

"And don't forget what he did to our picnic!" Scuttle added.

"But it's no fun when one of your friends is sad," Ariel said.

"I know!" said Flounder. "Maybe if Sandy and I asked him to play with us, it would give him his confidence back."

"Are you sure you want *me* to play?" Scales asked.

"Of course we do!" the little fish replied.

"Even after I made a mess of Sebastian's garden, and ruined the picnic?" Scales asked.

"Sure!" said Flounder. "You're our friend!"

"You can even serve first!" Sandy added, tossing the ball over the net to Scales.

Scales threw the ball high into the air. As it came down, he spun his tail around three times, then smacked the ball as hard as he could. But Scales's tail was very strong, so instead of just going over the net, the ball flew out of sight!

"This is terrible!" the dragon cried. "My tail ruined everything again!"
"It could have happened to anyone," Flounder said, trying to be helpful.
"I know!" Sandy said brightly. "I'll go find another ball, and then we can try again!"

"Please," the dragon said, wiping away a tear, "you'll have lots more fun without me. I just want to be alone."

"Our plan didn't work!" Flounder said as he explained to his friends about the ball. "Now Scales has gone home feeling even worse about himself."

"Hmmm," said Ariel, "this is serious. There has to be *something* we can do that will make Scales feel better."

"Scuttle!" Sebastian cried out as the bird flew overhead. "Come down here right now and help us think!"

"I am thinking!" Scuttle replied. "We birds do some of our best thinking when we're flying!"

Unfortunately, birds don't do their best flying when they're thinking. Soon Scuttle was tangled in Flounder and Sandy's net high above the ground.

"Scuttle!" Sebastian shouted. "Stop playing around and come help us think!"

"I can't," Scuttle cried. "I'm stuck!"

Scuttle certainly was stuck. And worst of all, no one could reach him.

"It's no use," Ariel said. "He's too high."

"What are we going to do now?" Sandy asked.

"He may be too high for *us* to reach," said Sebastian, "but *Scales* could reach him easily — with his tail!"

Sebastian scurried over to Scales's cave as fast as he could. "Scales!" he cried out. "Come quickly! We need your help!"

"Nobody needs me," the dragon replied glumly, still feeling sorry for himself. "Not with this big clumsy tail of mine."

"But that's why we do need you — because of your tail! Scuttle is caught in the net and you're the only one who can reach him!"

"Really?" Scales asked hopefully. "You need *me*?"

Sure enough, Scales was the only one who could rescue Scuttle. While the dragon gently pulled the net down toward the ground, Ariel and Sebastian untangled their feathered friend.

"I'm sorry I got mad at you about your tail before," Scuttle said when he was free again. "I guess it can be a pretty useful thing to have around after all."

Then the bird leaned over and whispered to Sebastian, "I had it planned this way all along. I knew getting stuck in the net was just the thing to boost Scales's confidence."

"Of course you did," Sebastian replied with a wink. "What a clever idea."

Scales grinned at all his friends. He was so happy to feel loved and needed again. "You see, Scales?" said the Little Mermaid. "Your tail may get in the way sometimes, but where would we — and especially Scuttle — be without it?"